W9-CPZ-774

DISCARDED

PATRICK'S
DINOSAURS

PATRICK'S

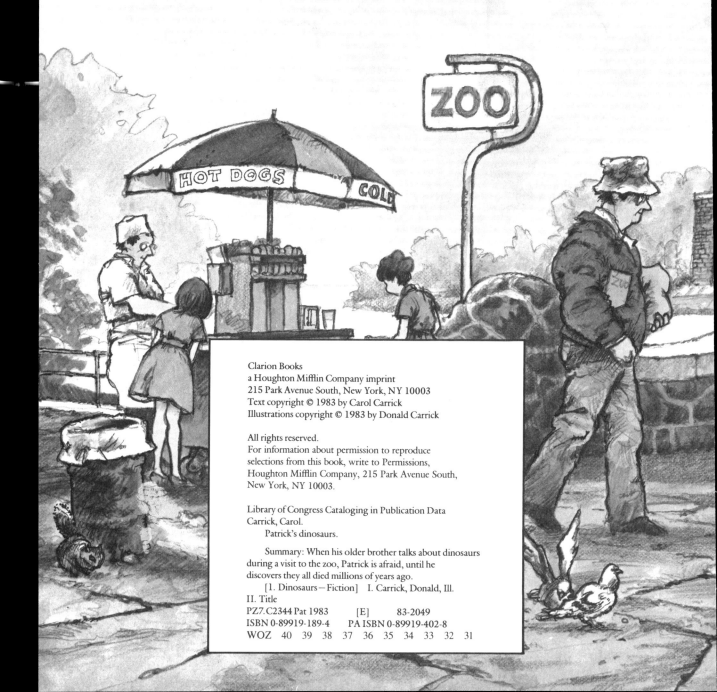

Clarion Books
a Houghton Mifflin Company imprint
215 Park Avenue South, New York, NY 10003
Text copyright © 1983 by Carol Carrick
Illustrations copyright © 1983 by Donald Carrick

All rights reserved.
For information about permission to reproduce
selections from this book, write to Permissions,
Houghton Mifflin Company, 215 Park Avenue South,
New York, NY 10003.

Library of Congress Cataloging in Publication Data
Carrick, Carol.
     Patrick's dinosaurs.

     Summary: When his older brother talks about dinosaurs
during a visit to the zoo, Patrick is afraid, until he
discovers they all died millions of years ago.
     [1. Dinosaurs — Fiction]   I. Carrick, Donald, Ill.
II. Title
PZ7.C2344 Pat 1983   [E]   83-2049
ISBN 0-89919-189-4   PA ISBN 0-89919-402-8
WOZ   40   39   38   37   36   35   34   33   32   31

DINOSAURS

By Carol Carrick ◊ Pictures by Donald Carrick

CLARION BOOKS/ NEW YORK

P atrick and his brother, Hank, went to the zoo on Saturday. They stood outside a tall fence and watched the elephants.

"I'll bet that elephant is the biggest animal in the whole world," said Patrick.

"You think he's big," Hank said. "A brontosaurus was heavier than TEN elephants."

"Gosh!" said Patrick. If Hank said so, it must be true. Hank knew all about dinosaurs. He knew more about everything because he was older and went to school already.

Patrick squeezed his eyes half shut. What would a dinosaur that weighed as much as ten elephants look like? The brontosaurus he imagined turned and looked right at him.

"Did a brontosaurus eat people?" he asked nervously.

"Just plants," answered Hank.

Patrick's dinosaur started eating leaves from one of the trees.

They went to see the crocodiles next. Crocs were Patrick's favorite because he liked to scare himself.

"Those are shrimpy," said Hank. "In the days of dinosaurs, crocodiles grew three times that big."

"Wow!" said Patrick.

"Just their JAWS were twice as big as you are," added Hank.

Patrick imagined an enormous crocodile. It was three times bigger than the other crocs. It was so big that it wanted the whole pool for itself.

The other crocodiles were too slow getting out. So the enormous crocodile opened its jaws that were twice as big as Patrick and gobbled them all up.

Patrick backed away. "We didn't see the monkeys yet."

After they had seen the monkeys and the seals, Patrick and Hank went for a row on the zoo lake.

Patrick looked down into the deep green water. What was that dark shape next to their boat? "Did dinosaurs know how to swim?" he asked.

"Some did," answered Hank. "Diplodocus, the longest dinosaur, could stay under water like a submarine because its nose was on top of its head."

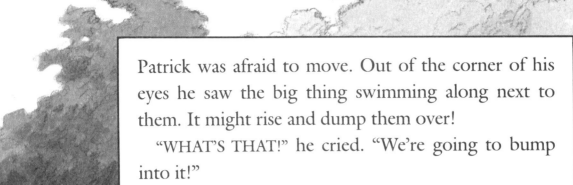

Patrick was afraid to move. Out of the corner of his eyes he saw the big thing swimming along next to them. It might rise and dump them over!

"WHAT'S THAT!" he cried. "We're going to bump into it!"

"No, dopey. That's just the shadow from our boat," Hank explained.

Patrick wasn't so sure. "Let's go home now," he said. "Rowing makes me tired."

When they got on the bus Patrick felt better, even though Hank was still showing off how much he knew about dinosaurs.

"A stegosaurus was bigger than one of those cars," Hank said. "But its brain was only the size of a walnut."

Patrick looked out the window. In his mind the lane of cars was a line of walnut-brained stegosauruses. The plates on their backs swayed like sails as they plodded along.

Hank reached up and rang the bell for the driver to stop. "A triceratops was tougher than a stegosaurus," he said. "It could even take on a tyrannosaurus."

The bus stopped at their corner. On the other side of the street Patrick thought he saw a triceratops waiting for the traffic light.

When Patrick and his brother climbed down from the bus, the hot dusty street became a prehistoric forest. Tropical birds screamed their warning. Too late. A dreadful tyrannosaurus crashed into the clearing.

Patrick held his breath as the triceratops lowered its huge head. Its horns pointed ahead like three enormous spears. When the traffic light changed, the triceratops charged.

"RUN!" Patrick yelled. He headed for their apartment building.

"What's the hurry?" called Hank.

Patrick didn't feel safe until the front door of the hall slammed shut. He wanted to look out his window, but first he had to ask Hank something.

"How big was a tyrannosaurus?"

"Big," said Hank.

"Up to the second floor, maybe?" asked Patrick.

"At least," Hank agreed.

"That's what I was afraid of," said Patrick.

He peeked into his bedroom. Sure enough, the ugly head of the tyrannosaurus almost filled his window.

The dinosaur opened its mouth to show teeth like daggers. Patrick didn't think this dinosaur ate leaves.

"Are you SURE there are no more dinosaurs around?" he asked Hank.

"Positive. The dinosaurs have been gone for sixty million years."

Patrick gave a sigh of relief. And the dinosaur
disappeared.